Mad Grandad AND THE
Mutant River

Can YOU spot
the mutant rat
hidden in the story?

*For all the teachers who helped
to make me what I am
(but it's not all their fault).*

Oisín McGann wrote and illustrated his first stories when he was about six years old. He loved books so much he wanted to make some of his own. As he got older, he was able to read longer and longer books, so he spent more and more time making up stories. After learning to write at school, he went to art college to learn how to draw and paint, but he still spent more and more time writing. He worked in lots of different jobs, like making cartoons and adverts, and his stories grew and grew.

Now he writes stories for a living, because he hasn't time to do anything else.

Oisín has made up more stuff about Lenny and his grandad in other *Mad Grandad Adventures.*

Mad Grandad AND THE

Mutant River

Oisín McGann

THE O'BRIEN PRESS
DUBLIN

This edition first published 2017.
First published 2005 by The O'Brien Press Ltd,
12 Terenure Road East, Rathgar, Dublin 6,
D06 HD27, Ireland.
Tel: +353 1 4923333; Fax: +353 1 4922777
E-mail: books@obrien.ie
Website: www.obrien.ie
The O'Brien Press is a member of Publishing Ireland.

ISBN: 978-1-84717-960-9

1 3 5 4 2
17 19 18

Editing, typesetting, layout, design: The O'Brien Press Ltd
Illustrations: Oisín McGann

Printed and bound by CPI Group (UK) Ltd, Croydon, CR0 4YY.
The paper in this book is produced using pulp from managed forests.

Published in

DUBLIN

UNESCO
City of Literature

CHAPTER 1

Grandad's Grappling Hook

I was on holidays from school, and
Grandad was taking me fishing.

Grandad was a bit **mad**.
He sometimes saw things that weren't
really there, or forgot what **year** it
was. But he was fun to hang around
with, and he had his own weird way
of fishing.

The other fishermen on the river were using fishing rods and nets, but not my Grandad.

He used a **grappling hook**. And he wasn't trying to catch fish, either.

We had pulled out loads of stuff that morning, like a rubber boot, a shopping trolley and even a bin bag full of baby's nappies. He said the river was better off without that kind of stuff.

'Oh, I've hooked something big this time!' Grandad called. 'Give me a hand, Lenny!'

I grabbed the rope and helped him pull in our catch. It was really **heavy**. As it rose up out of the water, we both stopped and stared.

It was a small **car**. Or at least it looked like a car. It had wheels, and windows, but it had fins too, and **propellers** at the back. There was a very annoyed-looking girl sitting in the driver's seat.

Or at least she looked like a girl. She had **fins** instead of ears, and a **tail** instead of legs.

'Look what you've done to my car!'
she shrieked.

The hook had punched right
through the front of it.

'It's a **mermaid**!' Grandad gasped.

'I'm nobody's **maid**, you great clod!' she retorted. 'I'm a **mer-model**! I'm Mari Aqua-Bella. I've been on the cover of *Splash*! magazine twice, and my daddy owns half the Atlantic Ocean! Now what are you going to do about my car?'

'We're sorry,' Grandad told her.
'Let me get that hook out, and then
maybe we can take the car to the
mechanic's.'

CHAPTER 2

The Big Bully Barry Cooder

As Grandad was pulling out the grappling hook, I noticed that some of the fishermen were looking our way.

One angler was staring at Mari. He was a **huge** man with a beard and hairy arms.

His name was Barry Cooder, and he was always down at the river, **bullying** everybody.

'Look at that for a fish!' he barked to the others. 'I've never seen one like it. It'll look great on the wall over my fireplace!'

'She's not a fish,' I said. 'She's a **mer-model**!'

'A fish is a fish!' Cooder snarled as he came towards us. 'And that one's mine! I wonder how much she weighs?'

'That's none of your **business** …'
Mari started to say, but stopped when
the angler cast his fishing line at her.

The hook was big and barbed and
sharp as a needle. It caught in Mari's
hair and she squealed as she was
yanked from the car by the fishing
line.

'Aagh! My HAIR!' she screeched.
'You beast!'

'Oi! Let her go!' Grandad shouted.

He grabbed the bag full of baby's **nappies** and emptied it over Cooder's head.

Mari picked one up and **slapped** the angler with it. Then she realised what it was, and dropped it with a squeal.

'**Fish-lovers**! I'll hook the lot of you!' the angler roared, his face screwed up in rage.

Throwing down his rod, he charged at us.

'He's gone **nuts**!' I yelled. 'Let's get out of here!'

There was nowhere to go but the river. I jumped into the driver's seat of Mari's car, and **revved** the engine.

Grandad and the mer-model squeezed in and she slammed the glass roof closed just before Cooder reached us. He hammered his fists on the glass.

'**Drive**!' Mari shrieked.

I spun the car around and drove straight down into the river. We sank into the water, rolling down the mucky riverbed.

CHAPTER 3

Weird Stuff Underwater

We rolled along the river bottom.

Fishing hooks dropped into the water above us, and we could see Cooder in his boat, buzzing back and forth, trying to find us. But the water was **green** and **muddy**, and his hooks only bounced and scratched along the top of the car.

'Mummy warned me this river was on the wrong side of the rocks,' Mari sobbed. 'I should have listened to her. Just look at my **hair**! I hope we don't run into any photographers.'

We drove on down the river. It was
a strange place, when you looked at
it from underneath. We passed old
bicycles, tractor tyres, and even the
rusting wreck of a car. Tree roots stuck
out like giant spiders, and there were
some very **weird** fish in the muddy
water.

'Wow!' I said, pointing. 'I've never seen a fish with that many eyes before. And what's that? It's like a **frog** with wings!'

'I see things like this when I eat
too much **sugar**,' Grandad told us. 'I
don't think rivers are supposed to look
like this.'

'It's all the stuff you
people throw in,' Mari sniffed.
'It makes the water funny. Everyone
says that humans are just slobs.'

We didn't say anything.

'I'll have to drop you off soon,' Mari told us. 'If I'm seen talking to somebody with *legs*, I'll just **die** with embarrassment!'

'Well, that's not very nice!' I
snapped. 'We saved you!'

'You dragged me out of the river on a hook!' she snapped back.

'She's right there, Lenny,' Grandad muttered.

We passed a large pipe that had sickly brown stuff coming out of it. As I looked into it, I thought I saw **something** move in the darkness.

I shivered and looked away. But then I turned back, just in time to see a huge, **ugly** shape burst from the pipe. With a crash, it rammed into the side of the car, and sent us tumbling through the mud.

The car ended up turned on its side
in a pile of rubbish, and we couldn't
roll it over.

We found ourselves staring into the face of the biggest, most **horrible** fish I'd ever seen.

CHAPTER 4

The Mutant Junkfish

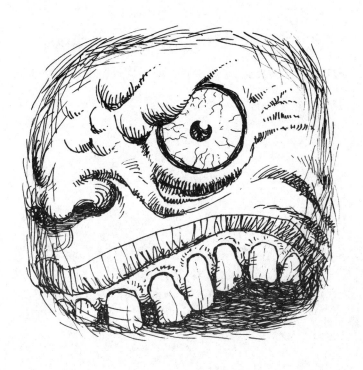

Imagine a fish that was ugly to start with, and then grew up in the nastiest part of a river full of junk.

Imagine it drank poison and ate garbage until it changed into an absolute **monster**. Then imagine it wanted to eat you. It had a hook on one fin, and a tongue like a tentacle, and chimneys on its back. It opened its massive jaws.

'I'm too young to die!' Mari wailed.
'And I'm wearing the **wrong clothes**!'

The junkfish's teeth banged off
the glass roof, and a crack appeared.
Water started to seep in.

'Hold your breath!' Grandad yelled.

'I don't need to, I'm a **mer-model**,'
Mari reminded him.

The junkfish **jammed** its hook into the crack in the glass and got a grip. With one tug, it pulled the roof right off the car, and water flooded in.

The fish pushed its head in towards
us, **gnashing** its teeth. But Grandad
was too quick for it; he reached down,
grabbed a car **tyre** lying in the mud,
and shoved it into the thing's mouth.

The tyre **jammed** there, holding the creature's jaws open. But it was still on top of us. We couldn't get out. The junkfish charged back towards us.

CHAPTER 5

Cooder Meets His Match

Grandad's grappling hook suddenly appeared out of nowhere and caught under the car. It started to haul us up the bank of the river.

Above the water, we could see
Barry Cooder leering down at us with
an evil grin as he dragged us out.

The junkfish had just managed to spit out the tyre, and was **racing** after us. If one of them didn't get us, the other would.

Cooder hauled us out of the water, but he still hadn't seen the huge fish.

'I'm sorry I was rude,' Mari said to us. 'I don't want to die a **rude** person.'

'Don't you worry,' Grandad grunted. 'That lad's about to get all the fish he can handle. Step on it, Lenny!'

The car's engine was still running, and I grabbed the wheel and stepped on the **accelerator**. We roared up the riverbank, and right past Cooder.

He was staring at us in shock when the junkfish burst from the water, and in seconds the two of them were locked in a **furious** fight. We skidded to a stop to watch.

'Those two deserve each other,'
Grandad said. 'I say we leave them
to it.'

'You saved my life!' Mari sighed.
'Not bad ... for people with legs.'

'Thanks a bunch,' I said.

She gave us both a fishy-smelling **kiss** on the cheek, and then hopped in her car.

With the Junkfish distracted by Cooder, the river was fairly **safe**. Mari waved to us, and drove back into the water. The car sank beneath the surface and headed downstream towards the sea.

We sat down and watched the fight for a while, and then had to drag Cooder away when it looked like the fish was going to eat him.

The Junkfish slid back into the river and disappeared.

It's probably still there today. And if you're ever down by that Mutant River, there's a chance you might see it, moving around, deep in the **murky** green water.